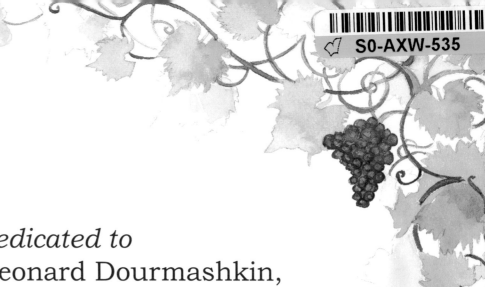

This Book is dedicated to
my parents Bernice and Leonard Dourmashkin,
to my family Geoffrey, Natasha, and Sarah,
and to the places on Martha's Vineyard that I love.

Poppy Press
3852 Camino de Solana
Sherman Oaks , CA, 91423

First published in the United States in 2013.
Library of Congress Cataloging-in-Publication Data
Dourmashkin-Case, Barbara
Pre press: Kurt Hathaway of Cartoon Balloons Studios
Printer: Benny Powell of Active Media in Claremont, Florida
Summary: Sarah, a little girl, ties her dog Peggy Day to the front porch of the Menemsha Market.
Peggy Day breaks loose and chases a kitten all over the beautiful island of Martha's Vineyard. Sarah is afraid
that she will never see her dog again when she thinks Peggy Day gets on a ferry headed for the mainland.
First American Edition - 2013
Printed in China

Poppy Press

To Katherine, Julian, Noah + Alma,

Peggy Day's Martha's Vineyard Adventure

love,

Written and Illustrated by
Barbara Dourmashkin

Barbara Dourmashkin

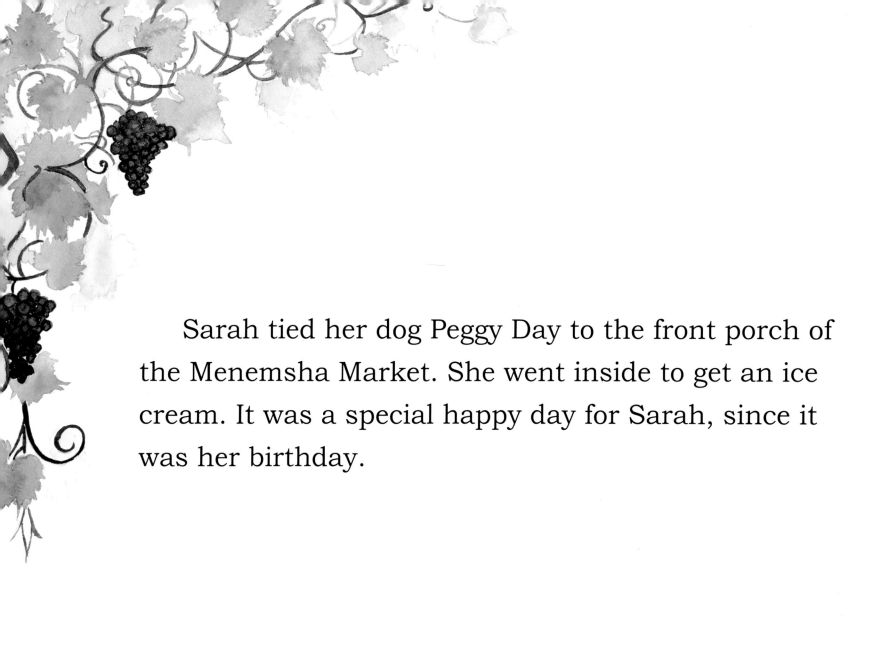

Sarah tied her dog Peggy Day to the front porch of the Menemsha Market. She went inside to get an ice cream. It was a special happy day for Sarah, since it was her birthday.

But all of a sudden Peggy Day broke loose and raced away, chasing a runaway kitten.

"Come back!" yelled Sarah, poking her head out of the front door.

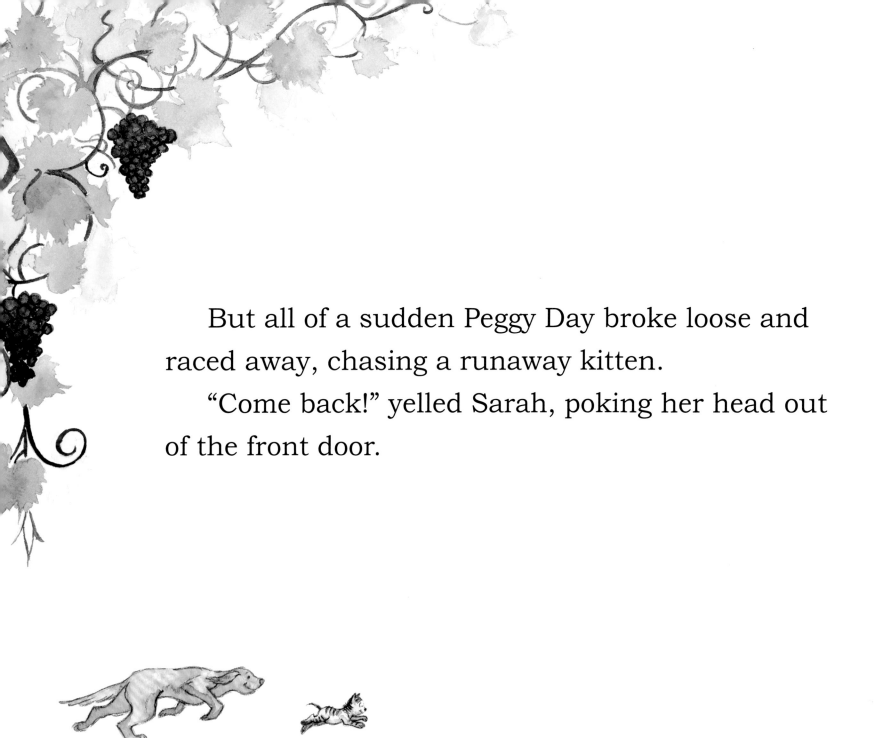

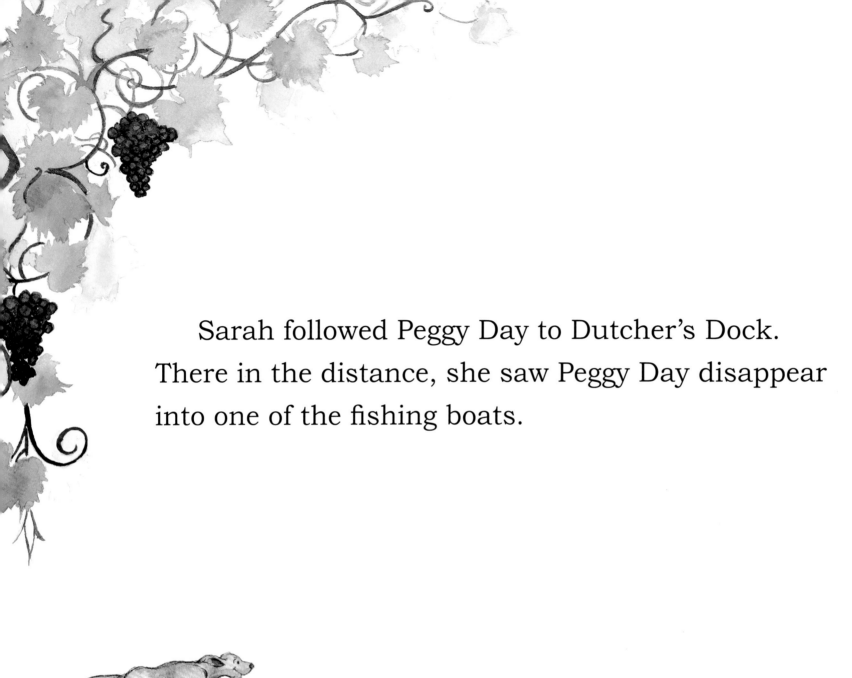

Sarah followed Peggy Day to Dutcher's Dock.
There in the distance, she saw Peggy Day disappear
into one of the fishing boats.

A fisherman was busy unloading the day's catch
of fish and lobsters.

"Have you seen a brown dog?" asked Sarah.

"Sorry, I haven't," said the fisherman.

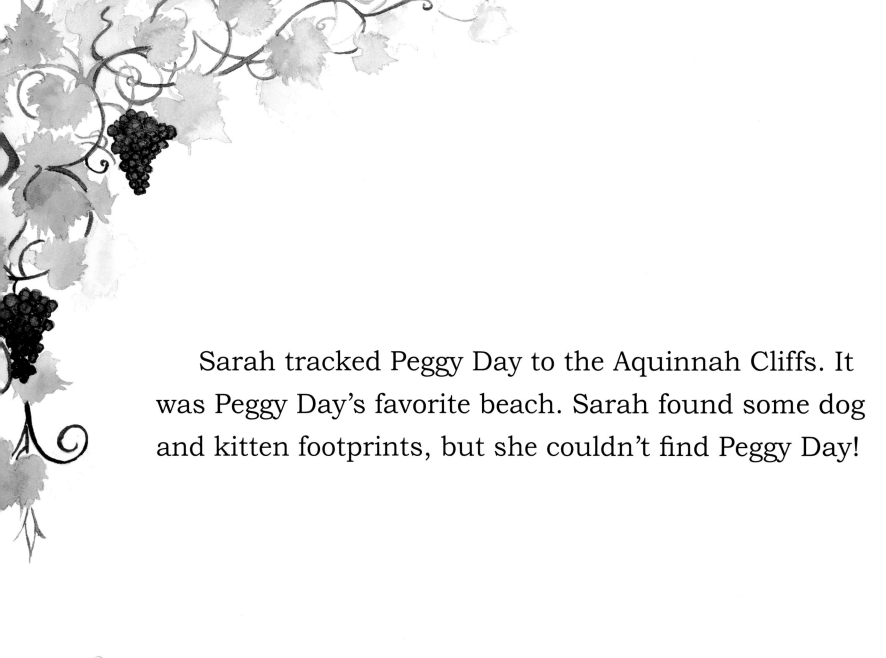

Sarah tracked Peggy Day to the Aquinnah Cliffs. It was Peggy Day's favorite beach. Sarah found some dog and kitten footprints, but she couldn't find Peggy Day!

Sarah followed the trail of footprints to the West Tisbury Agricultural fair, where a dog show was in progress. Running as fast as she could, Sarah almost caught up to Peggy Day. But before she could catch her, Peggy Day and the kitten ran away!

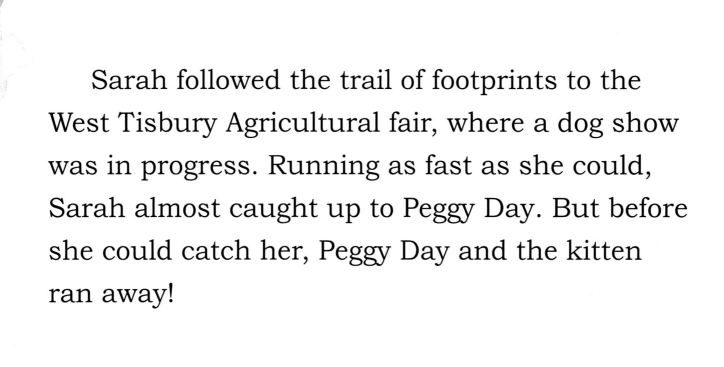

Sarah thought of all the places that she and Peggy Day liked to go.

"Of course!" she thought. "Maybe Peggy Day went to the Flying Horses in Oaks Bluffs."

Sarah was right! She found her chasing the kitten up the steps to her favorite merry-go-round.

Peggy Day was dashing around the merry-go-round chasing the runaway kitten. Sarah hopped up on one of the flying horses and reached for the metal rings each time as the carousel went around. Since there was only one brass ring, the lucky person who was able to grab it would win a ticket for a free ride.

"If I get the brass ring, I can stay on the merry-go-round and finally catch Peggy Day," Sarah thought. But Peggy Day and the kitten scampered off again!

Sarah followed Peggy Day to Edgartown. There was Peggy Day at the head of the Fourth of July parade on Main Street! But before Sarah could catch her, Peggy Day and the kitten escaped down the street!

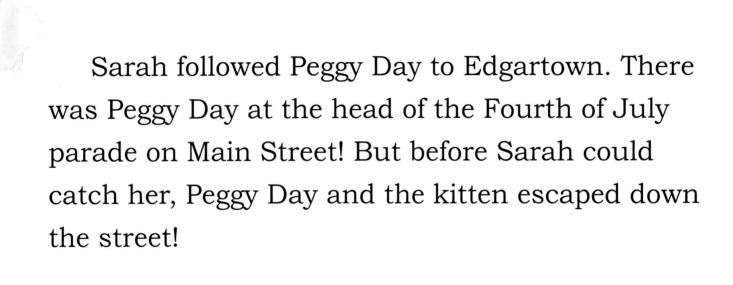

Sarah dashed to the ferry in Vineyard Haven, thinking that Peggy Day might be there. She saw a dog riding in the back of a pick-up truck that was getting on the ferry. Oh no! The dog looked just like Peggy Day.

"Come back!" yelled Sarah.

Sarah was very worried and sad. She thought that Peggy Day was on the ferry and she might never see her dog again.

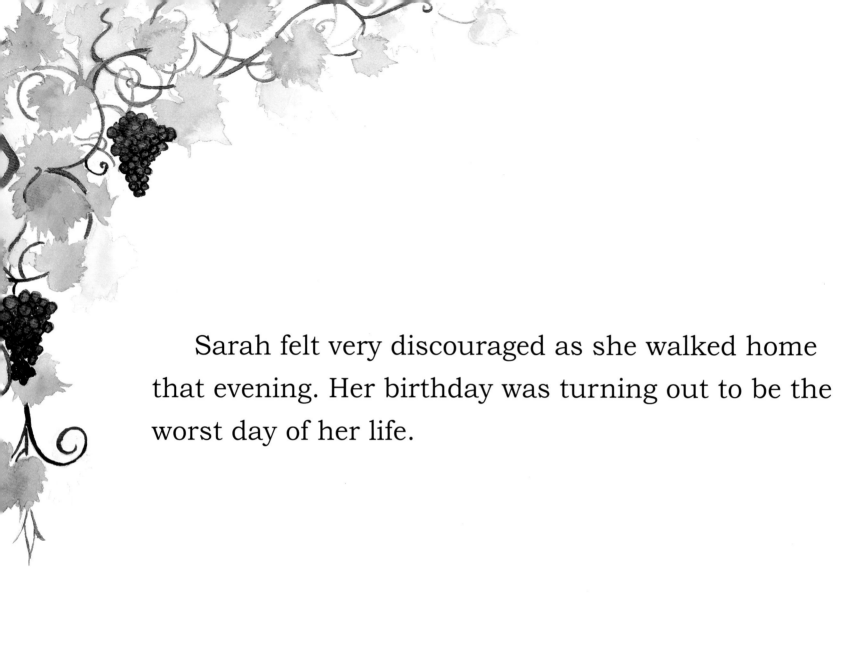

Sarah felt very discouraged as she walked home that evening. Her birthday was turning out to be the worst day of her life.

But when Sarah reached her front porch, there was Peggy Day!

Sarah was so glad that Peggy Day was home safe and sound. Guess what? Peggy Day just wanted to give the kitten to Sarah as a birthday present and that's why she chased the kitten all over Martha's Vineyard. Sarah realized that the dog that was getting on the ferry was a different dog after all. Peggy Day had chased the cat off the ferry and all the way home.

Sarah said, "My birthday has turned out to be a really great day after all!"

The End

Peggy Day photo by Peter Simon

Special Thanks to
Ann Arden
Laura Auerbach
Carol Bishop
Geoffrey Case
Wendy Grieb
Dorit Kassoy
Andrew Overtoom
Karen Peterson
Peter Simon
Stephanie Smith

★ Flip the bottom left corner of this book for animation of Peggy Day chasing the kitten.
★ Look for Peggy Day and the kitten in every picture.

West Tisbury

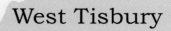

Menemsha

Aquinnah

Chilmark